D0323750

Dear Parent:
Your child's love of reading starts here!

Every child learns to read in a different way and at his or her own speed. Some go back and forth between reading levels and read favorite books again and again. Others read through each level in order. You can help your young reader improve and become more confident by encouraging his or her own interests and abilities. From books your child reads with you to the first books he or she reads alone, there are I Can Read Books for every stage of reading:

My First

SHARED READING
Basic language, word repetition, and whimsical illustrations, ideal for sharing with your emergent reader

1

BEGINNING READING
Short sentences, familiar words, and simple concepts for children eager to read on their own

2

READING WITH HELP
Engaging stories, longer sentences, and language play for developing readers

3

READING ALONE
Complex plots, challenging vocabulary, and high-interest topics for the independent reader

4

ADVANCED READING
Short paragraphs, chapters, and exciting themes for the perfect bridge to chapter books

I Can Read Books have introduced children to the joy of reading since 1957. Featuring award-winning authors and illustrators and a fabulous cast of beloved characters, I Can Read Books set the standard for beginning readers.

A lifetime of discovery begins with the magical words **"I Can Read!"**

Visit www.icanread.com for information on enriching your child's reading experience.

for Betsy and Rob Reid—
with love

HarperCollins®, ®, and I Can Read Book® are trademarks of HarperCollins Publishers.

Dinosaur Time Text copyright © 1974 by Margaret Parish Illustrations copyright © 1974 by Arnold Lobel All rights reserved. No part of this book may be used or reproduced in any manner whatsoever without written permission except in the case of brief quotations embodied in critical articles and reviews. Manufactured in China. For information address HarperCollins Children's Books, a division of HarperCollins Publishers, 10 East 53rd Street, New York, NY 10022. www.harpercollinschildrens.com

Library of Congress Catalog Card Number: 73-14331
ISBN-10: 0-06-444037-0 (pbk.) — ISBN-13: 978-0-06-444037-0 (pbk.)

❖

13 SCP 45 44

I Can Read!™

BEGINNING READING 1

DINOSAUR TIME

BY PEGGY PARISH
PICTURES BY ARNOLD LOBEL

HarperCollins*Publishers*

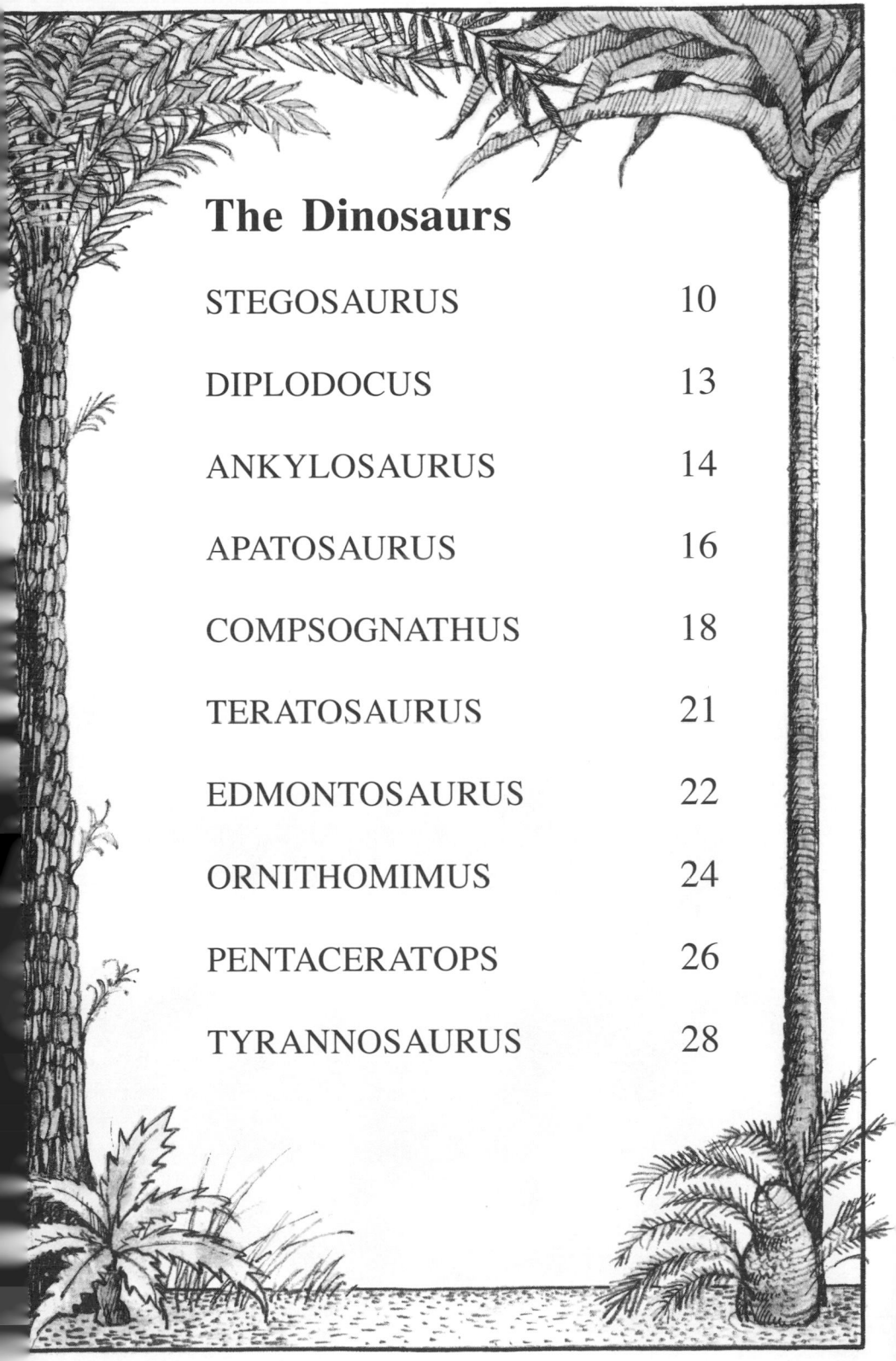

The Dinosaurs

STEGOSAURUS 10

DIPLODOCUS 13

ANKYLOSAURUS 14

APATOSAURUS 16

COMPSOGNATHUS 18

TERATOSAURUS 21

EDMONTOSAURUS 22

ORNITHOMIMUS 24

PENTACERATOPS 26

TYRANNOSAURUS 28

Long, long ago

the world was different.

More land was under water.

It was warm all the time.

And dinosaurs

were everywhere. . . .

There were big dinosaurs.

There were small ones.

There were fast dinosaurs,

and slow ones.

Some dinosaurs ate meat.

Some ate plants.

STEGOSAURUS

This is how you say it—

steg-uh-SAW-russ

This dinosaur

had plates on its back.

They were made of bone.

It had sharp points

on its tail.

It ate plants.

Its name is Stegosaurus.

DIPLODOCUS

This is how you say it—

dip-LAH-duh-cuss

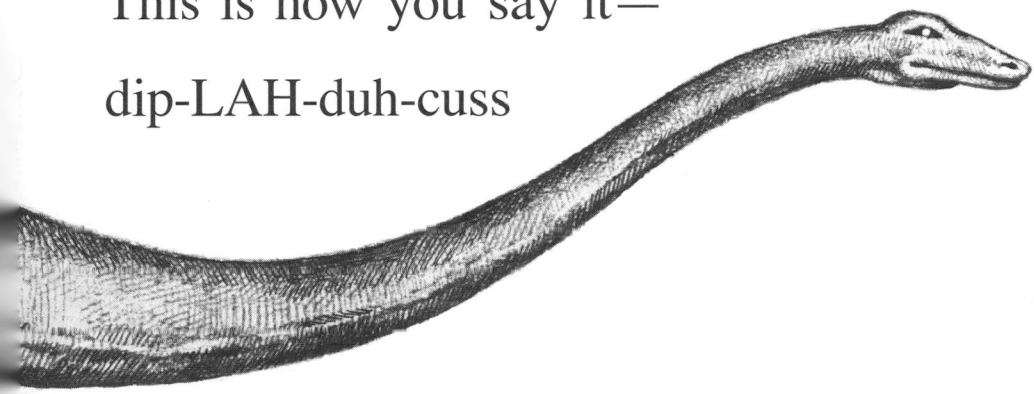

This dinosaur was long.

But most of it was neck and tail.

Its teeth were short and dull.

It ate plants.

Its name is Diplodocus.

ANKYLOSAURUS

This is how you say it—

ank-eye-loh-SAW-russ

This dinosaur

had a shell like a turtle.

Its tail was like a club.

Not many animals

could hurt it.

Its name is Ankylosaurus.

APATOSAURUS

This is how you say it—

a-PAT-uh-saw-russ

This dinosaur

was a giant.

But its mouth was tiny.

It ate plants.

It ate, and ate, and ate

to fill up its big body.

Its name is Apatosaurus.

COMPSOGNATHUS

This is how you say it—

comp-sog-NAYTH-uss

This dinosaur

was small.

It was as big as a cat.

But it could run fast.

It could catch other animals

and eat them.

Its name is Compsognathus.

TERATOSAURUS

This is how you say it—

tare-at-oh-SAW-russ

This animal

walked on its back legs.

It had big claws,

and sharp teeth.

It ate meat.

Its name is Teratosaurus.

EDMONTOSAURUS

This is how you say it—

ed-mon-toe-SAW-russ

This dinosaur

is called a "duckbill."

It had a beak like a duck.

Its beak had no teeth.

But its mouth did.

There were hundreds

of teeth in it!

Sometimes a tooth broke.

But that did not matter.

It could grow a new one.

Its name is Edmontosaurus.

ORNITHOMIMUS

This is how you say it—

or-nith-oh-MY-muss

This dinosaur had a beak, too.

But it had no teeth.

It ate small animals and insects.

Maybe it ate fruits

and dinosaur eggs, too.

But it had no teeth.

How did it eat?

A bird eats.

It has no teeth.

Maybe it ate

like a bird.

Its name is

Ornithomimus.

PENTACERATOPS

This is how you say it—

pen-tuh-SARE-ah-tops

This dinosaur had five horns.

They were all on its face.

Its name is Pentaceratops.

This name is just right.

It means "five-horns-on-the-face."

TYRANNOSAURUS

This is how you say it—

tih-ran-uh-SAW-russ

This dinosaur

was one of the biggest meat-eaters.

Its jaws were huge.

Its teeth were six inches long.

It ate other dinosaurs.

Its name is Tyrannosaurus.

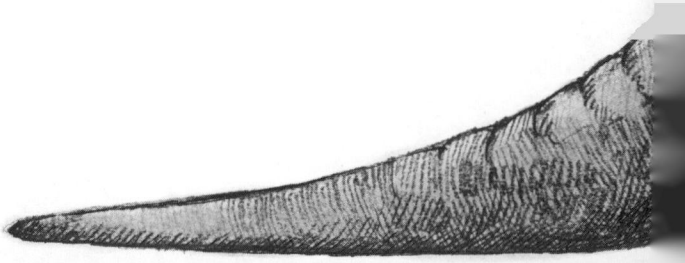

Dinosaurs lived everywhere

for a long time.

Then they died.

Nobody knows why.

But once it was their world.

It was dinosaur time.

AFTERWORD

A lot has changed since 1974. That is when *Dinosaur Time* was written. Scientists have found many more dinosaur bones and fossils. The tools that scientists use to study these artifacts are much more accurate than they used to be. In fact, most experts now agree that a major factor in the dinosaurs' extinction was an asteroid that hit our planet 65 million years ago.

We know a lot more about the different types of dinosaurs now too. For example, this picture of a Brachiosaurus from the original edition of *Dinosaur Time* shows the dinosaur living in water. In 1974, scientists thought that the Brachiosaurus lived in water because it was too heavy to run from its enemies. We now know that it did not live in the water, and even though it was one of the biggest dinosaurs and a plant eater, it was not too big to run!

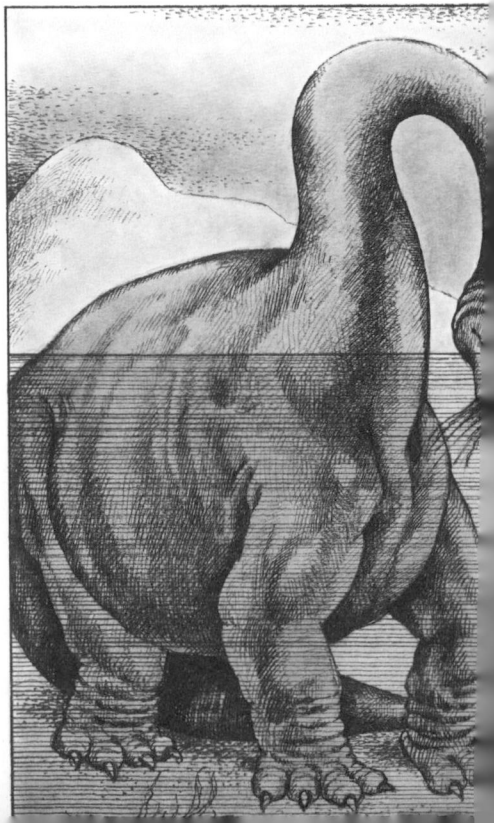

The dinosaurs became extinct long before humans were around to see them. Even with brilliant scientists learning more about these animals every year, we will probably never know everything about dinosaurs.